# MISCELLANEA

# Also by Charles D. Tarlton

*La Vida de Piedra y de Palabra* (2010)

Touching Fire (2018)

Get Up and Dance (2019)

Carmody and Blight: The Dialogues (2019)

Peaches and Roses: Poems on the Navajo Degradation (2021)

Littoral (2022)

Reflections on Edmund Burke (2022)

# MISCELLANEA
## POEMS

## CHARLES D. TARLTON

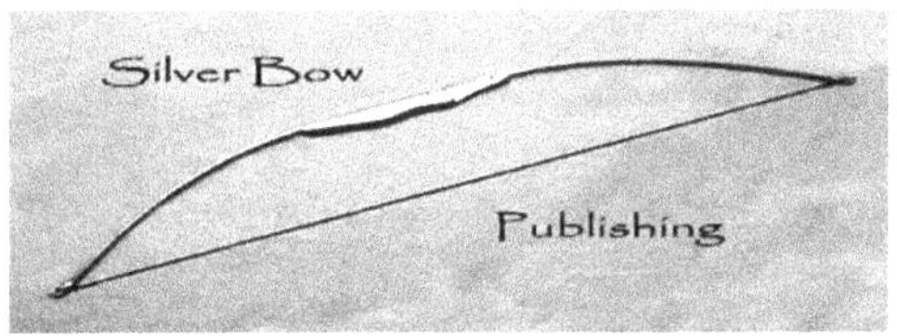


## 720 SIXTH STREET, UNIT # 5
## NEW WESTMINSTER, BC
## CANADA  V3L 3C5

Title: Miscellanea
Author: Charles D. Tarlton
Cover Art: "Red Painting Dream" painting by Ann Knickerbocker
Layout and Design: Candice James
Editor: Candice James



www.silverbowpublishing.com
info@silverbowpublishing.com
© Silver Bow Publishing 2021
9781774032558 Print
9781774032565 eBook

Library and Archives Canada Cataloguing in Publication

Title: Miscellanea : poems / Charles D. Tarlton.
Names: Tarlton, Charles D., 1937- author.
Identifiers: Canadiana (print) 20230216196 | Canadiana (ebook) 20230216226 | ISBN 9781774032558
   (softcover) | ISBN 9781774032565 (Kindle)
Classification: LCC PS3620.A79 M57 2023 | DDC 811/.6—dc23

For Candice James, *sine qua non*

# I. Verses

# II. Collaborations

# III. Longer Poems

# I. Verses

# Slow Awakening

*...things that in being real*
*Make any imaginings of them lesser things.*
                        **— Wallace Stevens**


My fingers sliding down the wooden banister
feel the corrugated grain of oak beneath,
                        and I think of barnacles
on the bottoms of sailboats up on stilts;
and when I break the mirror, its images spill
the way pearls fall from broken strings in movies.
                        They rattle on the floor.
Intangible *glockenspiel* are eager to be struck,
mallets poised, but the music's inchoate,
much of it unwritten, and the standing players
wait still for the cadence. Think of softness
in the embrace between the face that faces out
and the face that turns so shyly in,
                        guarding its secrets.

# Early This Morning

**with a sky wet as ocean
flowing with liquid slate
— Ezra Pound**

There was a moment, thin as a hair,
when the morning sun was waiting in the wings
and night gathered up her things to go,
in a preponderance of red, edged
in black, like a child's drawing
of a barn or a flower, the crayon rubbed
over and over along the border.
The first birdsong came just as the red
faded and the sun made a golden entrance.
A semi on the highway was changing gears
and its diesel engine roared like a bear.

# Reading the *Song of Solomon*

Take a blowing limb, bent in the wind
like the horns of a wild Connemara sheep,
and read your future from it.
                              Cloistered
singers next incant their brassy canticles
by *fishpools in Heshbon,*
                    *by the gate of Bath-rabbim*
in the lingering tide, in a crater-pool
made by rocks and mounded sand, where
a gull fishes for slippery bunker and tiny
crabs, the way one pecks and pesters endings.

Red clouds and black clouds are forming up
for reading, containing messages in code—
a face that runs like watercolor in the rain;
a ship on the horizon then dissolves;
and gold at sunrise in the leafless Maple limbs.
Down on your knees you're trying to reach
                    through, to take the bullet.

# The Poem Itself as Metaphor or,
# Is This Supposed to Mean Something?

*distant like castanets of antebellum teeth*
**—Tawanda Mulalu**

She dug so deeply into metaphors
there was no turning back, and had analogies
for everything she featured — books were
flutterings of leaves in a soft dry wind,
love was like rain or eleven on the clock, and truth
was a feather fallen from a flying gull
that fluttered noiseless to the ground.
                                                  She never
used one word when three or four
would do, and so her poems were long,
though none could really say they'd heard
any of it before.  She could dance around
grief (painted lady in her weird clown face)
or exaltation (on ladders up into the sky),
and prove whatever's in proximity's the same
as just-naturally-goes-with.
                                                And there are
nothing (look them up!) but perfect metaphors.

# Singing Rain

*..the windy sky*
*Cries out a literate despair*
**— Wallace Stevens**

The rain, gray up in the sky, writes
ditties down the cut-glass porch-door windows,
lachrymal its own lament.
                              The leafless
trees wave a thousand thousand long
skinny fingers wiggling at the sky,
in its indifference, hanging overhead.

The dream of the poem is to muster words
that are the same as things, and tie together hints
of a transcendent meaning; it counts
as music, the harsh kisses steely buffers make,
                              banging on the couplers.
We hung down on a dare, my brother and I,
from the wooden bridge over the river,
by our fingers, while the trolley passed by.

# Coastal Glimpse

***The sea was not, finally, my trade.***
**— Charles Olson**

The black outline of a bird's wings bending
across the sky above the sea makes me
want to be a seagull in a dream
of flying, see the world as if it were a map.
    I watch over my paper cup
the darkening shadows tether the clouds,
and bring them down close;
    how the bird can sail,
a tissue-paper kite in an erratic wind,
a dream escaping just as you wake.

## In this Light the Water's All So Blue

*The year grinds into ripeness*
*and rot...*
              **— Marge Piercy**

so leafless now, the elm reminds me,
when I had in summer heard
in the increasing dark
the wind off the Sound
strumming and rattling the leaves,
like the rustle of the snare
under the wispy brushes.

unheard, some unremembered
scuttling among the yellow'd leaves,
when: "There's nothing there,"
she kept insisting, "it's just the way
all the light's been drained away."
you would then say for certain
what's again been left unsaid.

he ran his little finger down along
the plaited coulees in the white ash's bark,
and strained to read the messages
carved there. He was the stylus wiggling
frequencies imbedded in the grooves,
and he made a music sylvan and spritely,
                  none but he could hear.

# Clinton Town Beach, Monday

***And now the STORM-BLAST came, and he
Was tyrannous and strong...***
**— Coleridge**

The Maple's blood-red leaves were first to fall,
then a cold rain came, and the blue and white fishing boats
stopped going out and coming in. There was no one
at the beach except a lone hispanic worker
parked there drinking coffee in his truck,
and watching the sun come up. *No soy nada mexicano,
soy de El Salvador.* Soon only the gulls would be here,
huddled, backs to the wind.
                        The silent message from the sea,
complete in itself, lay there now just beyond reach.
The Salvadoran's motor started, revved-up twice,
and then he drove away, up and over the old bridge,
and was gone.
                   There was a storm coming in, now
just a smoky line of distant clouds on the horizon,
but soon it would make the winds howl and the sea wrinkle,
fold and then unfold in rough corrugations,
                       rising up in the bay.
The bare masts in the marina signaled stiffly, dumb in a wind
that came in now under the storm,
                   black under the blackening sky.

# Clinton Town Beach, Tuesday

***The harsh acts of your levity!***
***Many and many--***
> **— Ezra Pound**

A single heron stood in a low tide pool
on a big sandbar all exposed by the tide
and, flapping heavily, she rose and glided
away in a whopping arc out to the empty
beach on the far side of the channel.
And the tide was so low the rubber float
that marked the water's depth lay like a drunk
thrown facedown on the sand.  Ornamental crows
hung in the trees.
                    *Caw! Caw!*
The tide far out exposed the sleepy beach,
the pace of things had slowed. Little boats hurried out,
the big yachts all sat heavy, tugging in their slips.
A single osprey wind-hovered past the sandbar,
glided in a long sweep, and then dropped
                    (O purist idea of dead weight!),
made a splash like a bomb might, and came up
                    with a fish and was gone.

# Clinton Town Beach, Wednesday

***...birds, leaves, snows***
***Order their populations forth,***
***And a cruel wind blows.***
**— Stanley Kunitz**

Mimicking the leafless Maples on Waterside Lane,
the parking lot was barren of cars as we drove in.
No one was walking a dog, or swinging on a swing,
or digging in the sand.
                          A single Whooping Crane
alighted on the nearby sand and waded in the shallows,
spearhead at the ready. Overhead, mottled seagulls flapped
and glided, this way and that, flew up onto a post,
then peeled off again, down to the sand, flew away,
and landed again.
                          Dark windows on Cedar Island
stared back at us, dull and sightless; docks and empty
boat slips grinned like missing teeth in a crooked smile.
In a steady stream, then, boats came out of the basin,
heading down to the sea, as if fleeing catastrophe.
I thought the rough stone jetty on the beach,
stranded by the tide, looked like a troglodyte giant,
                          exhausted, prostrate on the sand.
"A symbol, maybe," Ann said,  "that summer's over."

# Clinton Town Beach, Thursday

***There is the gale to urge behind***
***And bruit our singing down...***
**— Robert Frost**

It was dark, raining, and the sea was choppy.
In the parking lot and on the sand large puddles
mimicked the larger bay, and the wind blew wrinkles
on their surfaces and made the sea grass bend.

There were no boats going out of the harbor
and none at sea, just the lights in distant windows
of the *Old Harbor Marina*. The tide coming in
made the buoy at the boundary of the beach
bob and twitch. Fast gray clouds blew in
from Long Island. Two stubborn gulls
sat on the swing-shed's roof, facing into the wind
like mounted weather-vanes.
                              Far across the inlet
I watched a lone cormorant lift off and race
across to *Cedar Island,* never more than a foot above
the bay. The big *gneiss* rocks at the edge of the asphalt,
the thick plank fences marking the edge of the beach,
and the abandoned, sagging, wet, and unused
badminton net all cast faint cris-crossing shadows.
A sign forbidding the taking of shellfish had torn
                    loose, and flapped slowly in the wind.

# Beach Sand Formed By Erosion

***Take this Sea, whose diapason knells***
***On scrolls of silver snowy sentences,***
***— Hart Crane***

No great things but on the margin; such was
          the beginning of life.
Isolate and taking my own bearings,
I walked right up to the edge of the sea
and watched out over the waves as the tides
made even the great waters obey, heaving
like sloshings in the children's bath, the swash
sucking the sand down from the berm.

Oh, it is the stuff!  Bring in your microscope,
enlarge a grain, find light bejeweled there.

# The Black Dog Covid Song

*"The plague is come," a gnashing Madman said,*
*And laid him down straightway upon his bed.*
                    **— Christina Rossetti**

In parts of town where there have been the greatest
number of deaths from this contagion, witnesses all swear
they've seen black dogs hiding in the darkening shadows;
                    if you come close, they run away.

A dozen black dogs were seen in Fenwick, and another two
imagined at the Cove, a black ketch had been spied leaving
anchorage, and several people swore to God they'd seen
                    a black dog down by its mizzen.

I saw a black dog lie on a freshly filled grave
and he wouldn't leave. Then somebody told me how
two drunks down by the firehouse said they'd seen black dogs
                    flying across the face of the moon.

On the horizon just before dark, the sea was a mirror'd gray
and flat, Long Island like the desiccated, crumpled edge
of a dead leaf, blackening under a thin coating of snow.
                    The sounds of dog-paws digging in the dark.

Imagine a black dog, shaggy, desperate and wild, growing
like a hot air balloon, rising up and filling out above the fields
and up the sky, a swollen black moon of a dog,
                    blocking the bright white of the sun.

# *Apokalypsis*

***...there were once a million homes here,***
***and crimson towers along narrow lanes.***
**—Li Po**

The big and little creatures of the world, *en masse*
before the crumbling edifice whose walls erode
in acid rain; while we scurry away from Death's wheeze,
                    fingering our way along.

Plague after plague and the odds increase that something
final's bound to happen, maybe a crushing shock
that ends everything, lets in the beetles and the blow flies
                    to gnaw down our tallest towers.

Someone hesitates, a naïf, a wizened nun, a saint
frozen before the impending end of the world
who ignored already sounds of laughter and fright,
                    holding their ears, turning away.

Viral phantoms move misunderstood among us,
lay unseen along the ground, dance their *danse minutiae*,
deepening until we're sloshing through their toxin,
                    in our own immolating fevers.

# The White Cormorant: A COVID Mystique

*I walked alone*
*on the beach this morning, watching a cormorant*
*skid, thudding, into water. It dove down*
*into that shuddering darkness where we can't*
*breathe.*
**— Rosanna Warren**

The cormorant's a killer, a sleek stealth-submarine,
but the White Cormorant's divinity, a mythical bird.
Have you never heard of  it? They fly straight into the sun,
             carrying the inexplicably dead

like wavery ghosts in bleached percale. White Cormorants
tilt and dive for souls in the far reaches of the inky sea
that is the night sky, gliding between the stars.
                 Death's now pale, a widening sheet.

And what if I'm caught contriving this white raptorial,
making it up to camouflage a real wild virus?
I'm giving this rough pandemic a fanciful pale face,
                but it moves secretly already.

The White Cormorant sits on a rock, wings widely arched
to catch disseminating breezes; he's an anathema,
hovering over empty freeway rest stops, sneaking past
                 on currents around each closing door.

Does it legitimize contagium's grimly visit,
to make it something from the gods,
that stays just out of reach,
masquerading as a chalky, bleached divinity,
             a hoary *Phalacrocorax carbo*?

# Pungency

*When I follow after them,*
*The grass changes to stone.*
**— Theodore Roethke**

The older you get the closer you come
to the memory of things, to the history
in old houses along the shore, trees that distinguish
one town from another, and the moon that wades
in mystery.
        There's a scent and color
that drags us out of ourselves, but gradually,
as the years sand down the surfaces,
rubbing away once new and hot importances,
to bring us down to what's anciently vital
      — the gulls in the swash, or the moon.

## Under the Skin

*I keep no rank nor station.*
*Cured, I am frizzled, stale and small.*
**— Robert Lowell**

I walked onto the beach and sat right down to listen
to the wild waves hurtling in under the wind,
and I heard caterwauling, scornful things,
dark as the darkest clouds or blackest sea
and, in the distance, lost as if they'd come in
to the shore, glad and exhausted soldiers back
            home safe from their wild war.
A story's being told right here and the world's
pushing roughly in and mussing its hair,
crowding closer to hear.  The dark sea is full
            of clever things, a million images.

# In Little Things

> ***May you***
> ***sleep in sweet breath and***
> ***rise always in wonder...***
> **— Rita Dove**

Last Halloween's pumpkins are rotting now
where masked children poked and left them
                at the edge of the garden.
Their pulpy seeds and juice
fermenting now, making the last of the flies
drunk and stupid, like fools in love.

# After the Leaves Have Fallen

***And held in ice as dancers in a spell***
**— Richard Wilbur**

Under a rousing little wind,
tall white sycamores undulate
their gentle sinewy limbs
like Balinese dancers,
raising a basketful of questions.

Then an evergreen hedge, a palisade
of needles and small red berries
around a maple sapling, where
a lone *samara* once cavorted,
                    raising more.

# It's All Dance

*[T]he young people in the company and I are bodies together
making a body-based art form. It's hard.*
      **— Bill T. Jones**

Wispy clouds pirouette, tied to a blue topsail.
Garbagemen toss the heavy empty cans
over their shoulders, always keeping pace
                with the moving truck.
Stretched tendons and an archèd back, arms
                and legs shaved smooth,
the *primo ballerino* walks his tight line.
The sun overhead in a moment of cessation —
                *Swan Lake, Giselle, La Bayadère.*

# "Groping for Trout in a Peculiar River"

*...almighty Sex,*
*Go forth at nightfall crying like a cat.*
                    **— Edna St. Vincent Millay**

Daughters of Pandion, the swallow
and the nightingale, from retribution done
in fairly retribution.* Think of beauty, then, as food
and fuel to frenzy —
                    Tereus's and Giovanni's
heartfelt feasts.** What's an old head gone forgetful
and a younger empty at the start? Say clearest,
and not it's merely pale or glaring.  The searcher
peering under contrasts with the black lamb.
Half-naked in the car, in a memory of hot and wet,
and his frantic hands desperate. *Euhoe!!*

* Ovid, *Metamorphoses,* 6. 438-674.
** John Ford, *'Tis Pity She's a Whore*

## Stirred in the Heated Air

*It fills you with the soft*
*essence of vanished flowers*
               **— Mary Oliver**

"I loved the desert image from the start," she said,
standing by the gravel path from where you looked
down across the valley.
                    "See how the rain brought
out the shiny pink *Rock Purslane,* the redolent *Añañucas.*
O brilliant fuchsias, such fiery yellows!"
When, at last, the path reached the asphalt highway,
we were besieged by distillations of sage, a fragrance
so thickly sweet it was impossible to breathe,
      and we drove on through air viscid as honey.

# It's Just the Way of Things

*Foreground. Background.*
*What you can swing from.*
*— Renée Ashley*

They make the sky blue, the birds do
it, and they make the ocean blue and clouds white,
the sun in the morning just before it comes up,
and the last red rays of the sun going down,
        the way lines in a drawing lead us
by hints to find shadows in a leaf or face
in penciled hatch and crosshatch.

The things my father did and said
that made my mother cry soft, unheard cries
while he slept.
        A geometry of sorts, all
angles and tree leaves shuddering in the wind.

# Two Minutes on the Deck

*I forget silence
The owner of the smile.*
                    **— W. S. Merwin**

Say it was the last
yellow leaf on the last tree
and we were waiting for it to fall,
and for winter.
                    The sea's muted waves
couldn't be heard across the marsh;
they ran up, toppled, and fell back silently,
                    like William S. Hart
in a runaway stampede. Cyclonic clouds,
wind-twisted double stairways, winding
Long Island's crinkled brow,
          and the sky gone apathetic.

# A Matter of Time

*Time to plant tears, says the almanac.*
**— Elizabeth Bishop**

Time aches most when it's slow
in passing; its undulations make
you sleepy, like soft sand dunes can,
rolled over languidly by desert winds.

Years cluster like paper messages
blown up kite strings by the same wind,
       too far away now to read,
lost at the end of their wild tether.

# The Aesthetes

**Content is a glimpse.**
            **—Willem de Kooning**

The old woman leaned in closer to the painting,
              a bewildering disfigurement,
looking to hang her umbrella on something;
                            an orange sailboat,
in a twisted cadmium sun had found a hole
in the clouds exactly its own size to peer through,
the edges of its ruffled burning like wrinkling light
              *sur la frange de la rose.*

# Shadows

*The blackbird whistling*
*Or just after.*
        **— Wallace Stevens**

The shadow of one green bird flew over the land,
rose and fell with the land, thickened
and thinned with the land's
               dark wavy ribbon,
drawn by the green bird trailing charcoal.

A green bird flying over the sunless
land made no shadow, but was all the earth's
shadow. A green bird flies in and out
of the rain that falls from a small black
moving cloud. A licorice murmur of starlings,
their feathers greenly rainbowed,
         rises, twists, and swivels.

# Song

***Art marks the moment just before it flies.***
**— Peter Carmody**

Here's a rough disguise, a pair of feathered
wings, sharp talons, and a hookèd beak,
hanging on a stick in an old-coat scarecrow.

Wind blows sea shanties through the straw.

Behind the bright romance of the osprey,
the indistinct, the vague, the shadowy
thing concealed beneath a shroud, a line
drawn through an un-remembered line.

There was an audition and we read
each other's lines, made bird-talk, and lied.

# Was There a Date for the Apocalypse?

**For the mystery of iniquity doth already work.**
**— 2 Thessalonians 2:7**

*The world betrays all the shades of gray in morning light;*
*the sky a pseudo-silver up against the not-quite*
*blackness of the leafless trees. The clouds wander past,*
*and the sky coming through them is liquid mercury*
*running this way and that. Don't you want to know*
*what it means? What it might be?*
*Love that spreads or light illuminating prophecies*
*of something dire or (in another mood) desired—*
*the Second Coming, or just Tuesday.*

# The General Sense of an Ending

***What we call the beginning is often the end.***
***— T. S. Eliot***

How the sun was, how the light spread, mirrored
bright like silver on everything. The shapes
of houses outlined in the light, all angles
and planes, shaded kites and trapezoids
of depth were not illusions here, not illustrations,
but so real.
      A woman, dark, was standing there
and raised her arms, gathering in the silver radiance
like molten light, in drops and splatters off her eye,
wrinkling through her hair and in the leafless trees,
and ran away to the sea...the waves turned over silvery.
The woman was a poet and she drew us away, back
from the melting trees and from the sea. She didn't only sing
or promise, but there were also warnings there
that an end was near, how something was finishing,
      that we would need to find its meaning.

# Sing the Whiffenpoofs Assembled

*Ugliness was the one reality.*
        — Oscar Wilde

It was late in the city, and the harbor was oily,
driftwood lay random on the shingle beaches,
lobster pots, and blue plastic shards tossed off
here and there down near the high water mark.

Two boys in a dinghy drifted on the tide past
New Haven's "Pearl Harbor" (an extrados/box-girder
bridge) toward the open Sound, a Whistler nocturne,
shadowy and blue.
                    The poet parked his *Citroën*
nearby the muddy waters, saw the coal-fired
power station's shadow in the coming dark,
and threw his phrases, songful, to the wind.

Out on the highway, U.S. 95, traffic was snarled,
trucks and cars head-to-tails, everyone wanting
to slip their fetters and fly to the moon, fly,
                            fly to the moon.

# Preface to *Leaves of Grass*  1

Sweet, indolent and grandiose love, moist as morning's
dew on grass, he oozes from his carnal appetite
for everyone to see, and would persuade us this is best,
                    metaphorically, an expansive love.
The objects of his passion keep on rolling by,
a concupiscent cavalcade of the unwashed
                    and undiscriminating rabble,
starched stiff collars of the rich, and torn drawers
and soiled chemises of bold sinners.
                    His love is massive and voracious.

He comes on rude, bare-faced, and forward, standing in
for all the unexpressed, lecherous outpourings,
the inexpressible ones. He brushes close to me,
but I am too repelled by the sweet nectareous odor of his
sweat, how he claws
                    and clutches, twists in all directions.

## Preface to *Leaves of Grass,*  2

Hart Crane, Pound's *Cantos,* and Langston Hughes,
from Gwendolyn Brooks to *Howl,* Jean Toomer,  Eliot,
*Patterson* — all long poems owe Whitman —
                everyone's raking the *Leaves of Grass.*

Life's a hot endless quest (corny as it sounds)
where the poems open doors, kick us along down the road,
like tin cans or promises.
                Nothing's ever finished.

The greatest poem by the greatest poet's only an open door,
an empty elevator, the edge of a cliff, or a speeding car,
                where the risk's always great
and you live close to the bone.  Don't think you're alive
sound asleep, gathering your junk all around,
                snoring on your odds and ends.
Go somewhere strange, someplace different, let yourself be
                the odd man out, learn something new.

## Preface to *Leaves of Grass, 3*

She was a woman from over the seas, older,
                              raised in dark forests,
her teats withered and scarred from godly battles,
                              absorbed in lessons.
She told stories faded and muffled, the plots doddery.
                              We shake them off,
searching for new species, forms hitherto unheard,
                              unseen.

America held *Eleutheria*'s funeral,
and those there in attendance played
at being pallbearers,
                     but she pushed open the lid
and sat right up and gestured as if to bless
the congregated there,
                     and caught the eye
of the future's coming deities
                     — the wild frontiersmen, cowboys, factories,
                     and robber barons —

Inequality lingers like the smell of an old sweater.

## **Preface to *Leaves of Grass*, 4**

Beguiled madman of vague disorienting streets,
                    of thought cataracts,
who, being insane, mistakes the raging
                    of his hot heart for love!

From all the thrashing frenzies of history, he names
catastrophes, insanities,
                    a disturbèd world coming all undone.
He'd heard the thunder speak, the rumbling in the rocks,
                    wild in his wilder dreams.

The ceiling of the world cracks and opens up;
                    God's (or something else's) thunder
tears everything to pieces, rips the sky like tissue.
                    Our hero imagines he's the one
making these loud destructions, an ancient *djinn*
            playing with the smoky sky, and laughing.

Strapped to a wooden chair, his madness glowing
like a fever, he urges everything forward, makes long lists,
throws them aside, scratches theories in the dirt
with curlèd fingernails, "The devil's work," he yowls,
                    "the devil I tell you!"

47

# II. Collaborations

# "Carnation, Lily, Lily, Rose"*

Two girls lighting lanterns to reveal the lilies
                                    and the roses lost
in the end-of-the-day's darkening greenery;
everything's a metaphor. What do you make of a tree,
                  tall dark grass, or roses
blossoming out of the darkness, lanterns lit by innocence
and beauty? In the orange-tinted lanterns an electricity
glows, setting in turn alight
                              the cloud-fall of lilies, white
all across the top, the lilies like a rising flock
of snow-white fairy terns, we might see
against the dark that comes right after sunset.

What do you make of it, this *tableau vivant*
of little girls, flushed in lantern light,
                  their eyes demurely down, intent and innocent,
pure in their white bedclothes? So delicately the fingers
cradle the long tapers, the candle light tinting
their sweet innocent complexions, not exactly orange,
                  but the color of peaches.


*John Singer Sargent, *Carnation, Lily, Lily, Rose,* 1885-6, oil on canvas, 60 ½ x 68 ½ inches, Tate Britain. Public Domain. Can be viewed online at https://www.tate.org.uk/art/artworks/sargent-carnation-lily-lily-rose-n01615. The title comes from "The Wreath," by Joseph Mazzinghi, a pastoral glee for a trio of male voices, which mentions Flora who was wearing "A wreath around her head, around her head she wore, "Carnation, lily, lily, rose."

## Wunderlich*

Wiping dried polish from a tarnished silver *bain-marie,*
*rouge-andalou* bloodstains
                from the skirting of a prison hallway,
and an old sidewalk sanded, scraped, scoured, and abraded
         (try to work the essence of art in here).
"Tin," the workman said. "It's made of tin, like the old
fruit cans, pie plates, jugs and funnels." Twist
a bar of purest tin and it cries out
            —in pain or ecstasy, but who's to say?
Strings of bright red Chinese lanterns
    sketched roughly in the the brief, gray wind-rippled sea.
Imagine the slow junks, full battened sails on the Yangtze.
I see the clouds reflected, stretched and wrinkled,
              or maybe a dream of silverfish.

*Gerhardt Richter, *Cage (4)*, 2006, oil on canvas, 9 ft. 6$\frac{3}{16}$ in. x 9 ft. 6$\frac{3}{16}$ in., private collection. *Wunderlich* was a brand of pressed tin ceiling tiles manufactured in Australia. This painting can be viewed online:
htttps://www.metmuseum.org/art/collection/search/789681.

# En Voiture, Simone!*

Many houses are red, not the red
of ordinary bricks or the red of blood or cherries,
but the red of hot chili peppers
and the red of the cardinal
                   as he flashes through the yard.
The town's divided by the broken road,
        and all of the windows are dark, are flat
and dead and dark, as if no one lived there;
      it's just the idea, then, of a red town.

Notice, though, the leisurely clustering of green
             — green trees and hedges, grass,
green shadows on the leaf-stained road,
a pillared yellow rotunda with a green dome,
        and green fields persisting to the horizon.
Who would dare venture onto such a road,
       enter into all that candied color? Red burns
your eye, the green coolly oozes into every space.
We are roaring through, not daring to stare back.

*David Hockney, *The Road to York through Sledmere*, 1997, oil on
canvas, 48 x 60 inches, collection of the artist. This painting can be
viewed online at
https://www.hockney.com/index.php/works/paintings.

## Crow on a Cherry Branch*

The crow sits in the full blossoming tree, black
                          against white flowers,
portending darkness and magic in the images of new life.
             He hops up and down and against the wind,
an acrobat who somersaults on an arc of wing, a boomerang,
                   black and a high flier, now
weighing down the willowy branch, digging in
                          his *hallux* and *digit*.
As India ink is — black,  and as snow is — white,
                a black bird amongst the blossoms.
                          鴉 *karasu*
Nevermore: the black crow against the delicate stems
and flowers; sinister, his dark eye,
             bloody black against the flower's purity. Crows
can count odd and even numbers, even learn new words
                   and the rooks at Youghal hang like fruit
                   in the trees. I have seen fish crows in the swash
turning over shells, quarreling with the sanderlings
                                      and plovers.
Make up your strange stories, send in a mechanical crow,
             to measure it out, clickety-click, *Kraagh-Kraagh*.

*Ohara Koson, *Crow on a Cherry Branch*, c. 1910, ink and color
woodblock print on paper, 14.5 x  7.4 inches, Diakokuya. Public
Domain. This print can be viewed online at:
https://www.wikiart.org/en/ohara-koson/crow-on-a-cherry-branch.

# The Fan*

Before the quickened shuffle of her slippered feet, now
      softly still in the hush of an oriental boudoir
at the end of an anxious day, a sigh,
             and a welcome planned.
     She's waiting patiently for someone
we cannot know — her lover, as the artist has divulged —
        but now she calmly stares
      at the far cascading haiku on the wall
          壁に書く *kabe ni kaku*
Should we be allowed to imagine the lover? Will he be slim
      and mannered, perhaps a samurai
           with bellicose bravura,
handsome and heavily armed,
or a fat little rich man arriving in a palanquin
         on the shoulders of servants?
Is the writing on the scroll her own poetry, love haiku
      in a careful hand and graceful, too, as swirling
as *Hakujubo*'s on the wall?


*Katsushika Hokusai, *Woman Waiting for Her Lover* (1800-1805),
ink and color woodblock print on paper, (15 x 19⅛ inches) ,
inscribed poem by Hakujubo, Tobu Museum of Art, Tokyo. Public
Domain. This print can be viewed at
https://www.katsushikahokusai.org/Beauty-Awaiting-A-Lover.html.

# Overwhelmed*

As against death, life is so like that
bright blue
         and yellow against the snow,
on the trees, on the mountains, on the rooftops,
     as we wade through.
Nowhere around here does it snow like that;
         雪 *yuki*

a sprinkling, a dusting is all we ever get.
This is how the artist wanted us to feel cold,
to sense his dream of real cold, how doubt
in dark moments makes us feel
        cold and slumped over, limping
on our crutches, knee deep in our own snow.
When it snows the whole of things goes dark,
comes down close to the ground,
        is falling everywhere at once.
You'd never mistake real snow for stars
on a dark and starry night.
        The stars cannot
rain down upon us, do not really feel cold.


*Utagawa Hiroshige, *Evening Snow at Kanbara Station*, 1833-34, ink and color woodblock print on paper, 8⅞ x 13¾ inches, The Metropolitan Museum of Art. Public Domain. This print can be viewed at:
https://www.metmuseum.org/art/collection/search/36937.

# Lepidoptera*

Make it be what you need, stand firm, turn
black enamel and burnished gold into
                          the butterfly

           蝶 *chō*

had not the golden Swallowtail escaped,
    (*as per instructions, put the butterfly in its position,*
        *and pin down the delicate wings — push an insect pin*
*through the middle of the thorax, between the wings*
            *and mount it in the shadow box*),
had it been chloroformed exactly like the *Gros Ventre*
mannikins cooking cold buffalo over the flickering
colored lightbulbs and cellophane in the Indian Museum.
        O blasphemous destroyers, netted lunatics!


Perhaps the greatest artist could have caught
      the perfect patterns of the butterfly on the wing,
how it darts and somersaults, floats over and
        hovers along the spring afternoon, drawing
nectar from the lilac and hibiscus on its long
               curling proboscis,
and traced the delicate silken dry point of its oriental wings,
in mad patterns,
       arcs and Asian curlicues on my eye.


*Kubo Shunman, *Various Moths and Butterflies* (1880), 7¾ x 7⅞
inches, ink and color woodblock print on paper with poems by
Gurendo Nakakubo and Haikai Utaba, ~~Arthur M. Sackler Art
Museum~~. Public Domain. This print can be viewed online at:
https://ukiyo-e.org/image/japancoll/p245-shunman-butterflies-
8191.

## La Tempête*

Suppose it was an eye, a blue eye,
and those were crocodile tears
with an attached notice from above
                              ("long, heavy storms")
and, when the eye of the storm had passed
        everything went still, but perhaps a frightened bird,
its eye gone red, would whistle its tremulous song
                              across the flaxy marsh.


An opening in the cosmos made
                        by a blue star's dying,
cotton, corn, a roughly sawn pine board, the rocks
you find battling the relentless surf
                        in front of the Coast Guard House
in Narragansett.
                Gold filigree and the white caps
rushing through, the seagulls turning cartwheels
                              in the wind.


*Ann Knickerbocker, *The Storm at Montjean*, 2010, monotype,
collage and oil stick, 11 x 15 inches. Permissions have been
obtained for all of the paintings by Ann Knickerbocker.
Knickerbocker's paintings all can be viewed at:
AnnKnickerbocker.com.

# Fleurs and an Old Coffee Can*

The whole of the arrangement hangs suspended
                nowhere in the air, on *la corda di Arlecchino*,
                colored pink and blue *fleurs*
perfectly balanced on dry and twisted twigs.
Some hinted yet unfinished flowering on the left
                                laments the death of leaves,
while the blue coffee can nestles in, sprouting
                its very own bouquet, oblivious
as tin might ever be of foxtail *diaspore*.

Or it might mean nothing at all, just twisted ribbons
or some tendrils off the meandering sweet pea,
poppies, the wind-felled peonies, or pink
                                hydrangeas
cut and tied together in a weatherèd bouquet.
And, still, you keep reaching for interpretation,
you want it to have meaning outside mere anthology,
or just window dressing in some *chic boutique.*


*Ann Knickerbocker, *A Bouquet for Manet*, 2017, watercolor and
ink tense block on paper, 14 x 17 inches.

## **Incognitus***

Yellow, rising up in a pillar,
salt against a wounded moon, *aurora borealis* dressed
in full motley; think desert flowers, Oh, how the colors pour!
                    Reds and yellows, orange, and the blue
from a blue cleavèd porcelain vase.
Had there been smaller pictures
            lesser pictures, something denser,
                        in white and darkening blue,
within them, now sinking to a murky reddened blue and black,
red-orange lilies and the day's dusk peering out
or climbing out... I cannot fully enter in the heads of people,
            real or imaginary. The red glass,
the inky stains, the fractured vase.
                    I keep coming back to that.


*Ann Knickerbocker, *Porcelain with an Underglaze of Blue
Decoration*, 2022, Acrylic, collage, oil stick, grease pencil on wood,
40 x 30 inches.

# An Embroidered Corolla*

Like the eyes of a *Cosmo* model,
        her lashes long and dark
under the *yashmak* of a fashionable hat,
        (just wait for her to blink)
and a ragged snatch of netting, perhaps the maw
        of a billiards-table pocket
and somebody's blue jeans torn...but wait...
        is that the fire from a frightful cannon
just where I said her hat should be?

You'd think we were looking
into the dazzle of the sun through an ancient
        astronomer's filter...O Galileo!
And the frequency at which the flames
arise determines color,
                        makes the blue
Matterhorn rise up, the green expanse
of the Davis Strait, the Sea of Okhotsk,
        the black of a deadly adder or the turtle's
persistent progress.  And on and on,
the painted image leads us.
                Oh, make your mind up!


* Ann Knickerbocker, *By the Bridge at Ten-Shin,* 2021, mixed media
on Wood, 24 x 18 inches.

# III.

# Two Long Poems

# The Turn of Art:
# Five Dramatic Scenes in Verse*

*—for Janet C. Bishop, Thomas Weisel Family Curator
of Painting and Sculpture, SFMOMA.*

Scene: Gertrude Stein and Alice B. Toklas's *atelier* at 27 *rue
de Fleurus, Paris.*  It is 1907. The room is filled with heavy
furniture, a large writing desk, sideboards, tables, and
cupboards.

*1. PABLO PICASSO and HENRI MATISSE sit in low chairs across
from each other in front of a fireplace.  They face us as if
looking into a camera (think of the famous photo of Gertrude
Stein and Alice B. Toklas taken by Man Ray in 1922).*

> On the wall behind PICASSO, five MATISSE paintings
> are hanging — *Woman in a hat (1905), Madame
> Matisse (1905), Le Bonheur de vivre (1905-6), Blue
> Nude (1907), and Self-portrait (1906).*
>
> On the wall behind MATISSE, we see five PICASSO
> paintings—*Boy Leading a Horse (1905-6), Gertrude
> Stein (1905-6), Young Acrobat on a Ball (1905), Nude
> with Joined Hands (1906), and Self-portrait (1906).*

**PICASSO**
once we had turned
our backs on the museums

> *Pause.*

where could we go?

> Indicates **MATISSE,** sardonically.

then *he* started drawing
lines of paint an inch wide

**MATISSE**
wasn't easy
while so many others
were portraying

the fine veins of a nose
details in strands of hair

**PICASSO**
not enough, not
for him, just to make it
look like real fruit

> *Pause.*

no more *trompe-l'œil* for him

> *Pause.*

a dot's enough for a nipple

**MATISSE**
I drew with brush-
loads of flat blue house paint
made my lines thick
all around the outside
black between trees and sky

> *Pause.*

> **MATISSE** stands and crosses the room.  He takes
> *Boy Leading a Horse* from the wall and carries it
> back to his chair.  He leans it against the wall
> beside his chair and sits down.

Not everyone, however, followed my lead.

> *Pause,* admiring **PICASSO's** picture.

browns and some grays

this is a precocious child's
drawing.  A horse!

a boy's dream of the West
wide open plains to ride

**PICASSO**
a poetic
dream might more easily
bring in the cash—

hung on Gertrude's wall till 1913
you often saw it there

      *Pause,* **PICASSO** points to a spot on the wall

later Nazis forced
*von Mendelssohn-Bartholdy*
to liquidate
*hispano-judaic*
art, smuggled out and sold

**MATISSE**
marketable
like pigeons in St Marks
swarmed around you
as they changed to property
they escaped like wild birds

      *Pause.*

I was waiting
for you to drop it all
come up to art
renounce celebrity
stop showing off—show us!

      *Pause.*

works of genius
make us feel supremely

diminutive

genius has to give it up
forfeit its advantage

**PICASSO**
has to give up what?

**MATISSE**
superiority

> *Pause.*

they used to say
I wish I could draw like that

> *Pause.*

now they say, anyone could

> *Pause.*

**PICASSO**
I felt deeply
every brush stroke, each of these
as I made them

> *Pause.*

but in cold aftermath
brought just financial success

> *Pause, as if reflecting.*

I was watching, you know, despite my cool demeanor.  But, I
loved that life in the cafés, you know, the money, spreading

my name around.  And the women, they all wanted to touch
my genius.

> *Pause. To Matisse*

You did none of that.  You ran no races, gave no quarter. How
was that? You were ahead, tossing off thick-limbed monsters
driving me mad. You made these obstacles I had to climb
over.

**MATISSE**
Finally!

**PICASSO**
I wanted to paint
with a heavier hand

lose all my fear
of teachers, my father

forget about the saints

**MATISSE**
could see clearly
down into the world's heart
below surfaces

but you kept painting them,
the surfaces, the smiles

> **PICASSO** stands and claps.  He then crosses
> the room behind **MATISSE** and removes *Woman
> with a Hat* and carries it back to his chair and
> holds it on his lap, partly turning it so the audience
> can see.

**PICASSO**
this is, of course
all odd lumps of color
unexpected

rub out the woman's face

    **PICASSO** covers the face with his hand.

—and behold Kandinsky!

you sped ahead
on wings of distortion

shape and color
yours to waste, invent
new wonders for the eye

    *Pause.*

no milliner
could make a hat like that

it was conceived
on an insane palette
laughing, you were laughing

    **MATISSE** looks around the room, as if trying to orient
    himself.  Coughs.

**MATISSE**
Somewhere near here, art's roadmap changed abruptly.  Up
ahead or looking just behind us, out of the corner of my eye,
we were poking forward, looking for the line just so we could
step over it.  I saw you coming up.

**PICASSO**
the other side,
how I longed to be free

overstepping
there'd be no looking back

**MATISSE**
make the first *real* pictures!


**2**. *The stage goes dark.  Under a single spot, two middle-aged
men emerge from the wings,* **PETER CARMODY** *dressed as*
**GERTRUDE STEIN and ANDREW BLIGHT** *as* **ALICE B. TOKLAS,**
*wearing the same hats worn in the famous snapshot taken in
Aix-les-Bains, 1927.*


**CARMODY (as GERTRUDE)**
they never knew
what the very next thing

might be—tiny

legs, an arm, both thick as trees
palm tree fronds like fish bones


**BLIGHT (as ALICE)**
They were always searching
for it, for the new thing.  At first
in different ways; Picasso,
of course, classically trained,
gifted, was a long time shaking off

the lessons, his tutored
instincts.  Blue and Rose periods
—could have been using a camera.

      *Pause.*

Henri was different, all for
crude outlines, sudden colors,
rough dabs of paint,
the merest suggestion.


**CARMODY**
he made it strange
defied the viewer's eye

**BLIGHT**
no matter what
it was, it disappeared

**CARMODY**
into paint, just the paint

>	*Pause.*

That's it, of course.  He overthrew the subject. Only the paint counted. That was where the eye fell; there, on the paint, the thick paint piling up, the paint on top of other paint, the paint plowed by the brush like a field readied for planting.

>	*Pause.*

Look on the wall!  You see the picture of his wife, *Madame Matisse*, with the green line down her nose?

>	*Pause.*

See what I mean?

>	*Pause.*

Compare that to Picasso; choose one there on the wall. What about the portrait of *Gertrude Stein?*

>	*Pause.*

...*my* portrait.

>	**PICASSO and MATISSE** rise and retrieve their
>	respective paintings and bring them down.
>	They stand under the spot, holding the paintings
>	in front of their chests.

**BLIGHT**
He meant it to look like you, a *resemblance*, but he said, if it
didn't look like you right now, that was all right, because it
eventually would.

**CARMODY**
...exactly me.

>	**PICASSO** holds the painting out and turns
>	it so he can see it.

**BLIGHT**
...or looks like you

>	*Pause.*

he was looking for truth
not just surfaces
behind those eyes, a mind
was watching for a sign

**CARMODY**
You're right, I had already seen so much.  So, I was always
waiting, it seemed.

>	*Pauses, musing.*

...on the lookout

**BLIGHT**
your eyes reach out to probe what you're hearing, as if to say,
I had hoped you'd not be like the rest.

**CARMODY**
And, what do we say about *Madame Matisse*'s portrait?  Can
your discerning eye probe deeper meaning there?  What do
you make of that green stripe?

**BLIGHT**
perhaps he meant

only to encompass
her, register
her contribution to life—
camaraderie in a wife

**BLIGHT**
How could we ever know?  No painting "means," not in that
sense.  The planes, the bumps, the scraggly lines, the lumps
of paint, the tiny brush stroke out of place, lock on the eye,
forbid the brain.

**CARMODY**
I still say it's not just paint; the spirits of all the wild emotions
caught up in spread colors, bone splinters in the *ambergris*—
tint, thickness, smell—wide brushes.

It looks like whatever you want it to look like.

> *Pause.*

**BLIGHT**
No.  It was not about looking, or smelling, or being *like*
anything at all.

It meant in fact—red, the green, the violet, and orange; just as
it means blue, black, and yellow—in any of their many
permutations, in a chance encounter, as crude parts of the
world.

> *Pause.*

The flowers ripped from the earth.

> *Pause.*

> **PICASSO and MATISSE** come forward and speak.

**MATISSE**
it was to paint
because I was making

**PICASSO**
objects from paint

       *Pause.*

my mind's eye gave the world
only the quickest glance

**CARMODY AND BLIGHT** exit.


**3.** Spot off, stage lights up. **MATISSE and PICASSO** go back to
their chairs. **PICASSO** points up at his painting, *The Young
Acrobat on a Ball.*

**MATISSE**
there's a story
in that one for certain
pure narrative
focuses attention
on our uncertainty

**PICASSO**
it was Giotto

(or me) could draw perfect
freehand circles

**MATISSE**
painted like Velázquez
aims now to be a child

       **MATISSE** crosses the room and stands
       under his painting, *Le Bonheur de Vivre.*
       He points up to it.

**PICASSO**
Childishness, to be sure, yet there's nothing *childish* about it,
at all.

*Pause.*

Your hills and distances are but suggested (did you notice?),
while the big ideas, all the rest, are wild reds and greens,
hints of mythology in all the playful poses; they have only
circles and careless dots for eyes, spring frolics, and a touch
of sensuousness, perspective out of whack — verges on the
humorous.

*Pause.*

Far more expressive than my pouting giant or my morose pale
hills.  Your lovers run in search of cartoon nudity.

**MATISSE**
So, you want to talk about nudes?

> **MATISSE** reaches up and removes Picasso's *Nude with
> Joined Hands*.  He looks closely at it.

You were still painting like Velázquez.

*Pause.*

you're so polite
your nude's too well-mannered
covers herself

could be from Pompei's walls
a goddess or priestess

she's a mural
painted on Spanish stucco
inside a church

**PICASSO**
I meant to make women
of paint someone could love

I was out to show the world who was master.  Infinite reflection and dark resignation show on the faces of my men; the deepest sadness, calm, or joy appears on the faces of my women, because they are so beautiful.  The children know so much.

I could not paint the kind of pulsing stones, the female boulders you were so happy to make.

> *Pause.*

I dreamt women
you could take out walking
they'd hold your arm

it took time seeing how
wrong I was; took longer catching up.


**4. PICASSO** goes behind his chair and takes out a long pointer rod.  He goes over to the paintings and stands in front of *Blue Nude*.  He points up to it.

> *Long Pause.*  He is just looking at the
> painting, transfixed for a moment.

**PICASSO**
this was vulgar
so I at first decided

androgynous
whore-sailor all in one

promiscuously drawn

> *Pauses* again, and leans intimately
> toward the audience, in confidence.
> Speaks very slowly.

Porn...o...gra...phic!-

*Pause,* sighs in resignation.

this beautiful hulk is
REALITY

Look at it!  Look at it!
hips, ankles, twisted rib cage

    *Pause,* to **MATISSE** directly as if, for
    the moment, giving in.

This was your high water mark.  I knew it instantly.  I ran home
and drew a hundred chunky naked women leaning on their
elbows, sharp hipbones and one leg flung over the other—a
hundred, at least.

You had launched a thunderbolt, for certain, but I thought to
myself, "I can rise to that, I will rise up to that!"

**MATISSE**
caught by surprise
lost sight of the way ahead
in a fever to catch up

    *Pause.*

with this the history
of modern art resumes
that we could teach
the art world to embrace
this meaty toad

love and art together
move closer to the truth

**PICASSO**
The way ahead congealed,
the compass and the raw materials were set.

    *Pause.*

Forward!

**MATISSE**

    *Pause,* indicating the *atelier,* the walls,
    the furniture.

If anyone could have seen into the future, this would have
been the place...

    Makes an all-inclusive gesture with his
    waving arm.

...where it all started.


**5. PICASSO** reaches up and takes down the *Self-portrait* by
MATISSE; MATISSE takes down the *Self-portrait* by PICASSO.
They both come forward and stand holding the paintings and
facing the audience.  PICASSO pulls a false beard from the
portrait of MATISSE.  The two portraits reveal a strong family
resemblance—the portraits of two brothers.

*Curtain*

* "The Turn of Art: Five Dramatic Scenes in Prose and Verse,"
first appeared in *Fiction international 45,* "About Seeing,"
Fall, 2012. The photo can be viewed at
http://fashionhistorian.net/blog/2011/05/12/image-
making-gertrude-stein-and-venice-incognito/

# The Saga of the Rock in the Jar*

## 1

your eye catches it
unexpectedly, a straggly fugitive
detail amidst the forest's
disarray, illogical and off-hand
in a glimpse of sun down through
a brushy filter of pine.
just a small irregular rock,
glassy blue, and subtly blurred
below the currents of a mountain
creek, somewhere off the road.

not at all auspicious, this rock,
water pocked and angular,
the underside a flatly polished
mica sliver of sky, grey
on the upwards.  A rock gone
unnoticed other than obliquely
by the odd skittish deer come
for a drink, or raucous blue
jays stirring up a bath.

now, visualize this rock
in the palm of your hand, destined
for the jar of souvenir seashells;
see reflected in it now
your own scrutinizing glances,
the very backdrop of sky and cloud
you're standing in.  It goes
in your pocket, clicking up
against a penny and a quarter.

once home, emptying your treasure
on the kitchen table, you laugh,
coming upon the little rock,
and drop it in the jar
of seashells.  It alters everything;

its mirror refracts the crowded
seashore contents of the jar.
                              The shells
roll over and roll their eyes.


**2**


*"every vacation from now on,"*
you had said, on that last day at the beach,
*"we'll come back here and add more
seashells to the jar.*
                    *A sort of observance."*

notice the clumsy, lopsided
collisions the rock makes against
the smooth parabolas and ampersands,
the swirled edges, and thin ridges
of the lustrous shells. Turn the jar
in your hands, and the tumbling
upstart rock reveals the graceful
seashells to themselves. Mother
of pearl discovering its own
reflection in the watery isinglass;
the rock wears their likenesses,
disguising the dissonance.


**3**


the red and yellow kitchen walls
awake and indicate the scene;
a roomful of common objects
strategically pinpointed
like sectors of an artillery map,
imagined ribbons stretched in a geometry
and fastened to thumbtacks,
the battle of ontological
vectors joined.

New truths revolve
in the room, the jar and the rock
and shells arc along the compass,
projecting, like a mirrored disco ball,
the center out to the periphery.

The increase
of distance and angular rotation
throw rock and shells against each
other lewdly. They exchange
expectant kisses in the jar
and the jar caresses them.

This dumb
subversive rock has brought
the windows in, and with the windows,
trees as well as sky.  No glass
confines its movements, the rock
sees at the speed of light.

with the seashells in the jar,
the jar centers the kitchen,
surrounded by yellows and reds,
the colors spreading inward and out;
the rock greedy, the rock coquettish,
looking past the kitchen
and its own projected kitchens
into the trees and clouds.

what does its cold eye remember?


**4**


not ever being born, the rock
knows nothing about ripening,
or the fluctuations of growth emerging
ahead of the blood's vulgar spurts;
it assumes only sameness, always the one
thing. The water lay over it,

beyond the water, light and dark,
blue sky in its stillness,
clouds slow, white or gray,
and the glaring sun.
The rock had no
organic ties, no family; it was a chip
randomly broken from some larger rock.

memory was of no consequence to it,
nothing grew or passed through it.

geometry and physics were its genesis,
whose forms are over and over
seeded, crystallized, and dumbly cleft
(no *massif* could ever conceive, gestate,
or bear pebbles in its image.
no boulder promiscuously unrolls
green tendrils to bind itself
to fences.

      Now, the rock finds
itself revised; it can smell the ocean
on the shells, the hints of flesh
in the wet jar, a salt sea stink
unknown amongst the magma and mineral
upheavals, the slow stony stew
from which he came.
          A real novelty,
this rock, burly adjacent
to the daintier seashells,
exhibiting traces how they once
were hinged to allow life to pump
in and out, where they could hide
from the light itself, or wear rings
marking how they grew, were used,
and had aged.

      The rock cannot grow,
but only be worn down, roughly gouged
across its glassy eye, or broken.

past the shells and the kitchen
implements, the rock records the sky,
exploring how to seize the garden,
and bring it all in, to catalogue
the exuberant and unfamiliar
flowers, combing the saw-tooth
of picket fence for new theorems.
gathering as it goes along,
it wants to teach the shells more
than the walls, to reveal the widening
circumstances *a propos* themselves,
to show them to the moon.


**5**


nothing waits behind these
reflections but impenetrable
crystal; how a little rock contains
the world. Everything adds up

—shells, walls, windows, trees,
fence, clouds, and the sky,
as far as the eye can see into
the little retina in the jar.

but the rock still knows nothing.
no time passes there, though movement
and stillness come and go and rest.

inertia, wound up or disengaged
like a broken watch spring,
metes out random, uncalibrated
distances and speeds.
                              (Time
should be able to record
something meaningful).  All the things
inside and out are sizing
one another up according to weight

and their proximity;
they go fast or slow, ardently
awaiting or tense with dread
for something to come around
again, make any of it matter.

we will keep vigil out
our windows, throw one another
censorious looks, tragic
to comic, in the to and fro.
scenes projected on the rock's
cinematic surface need more
than what the reflecting
unreflective little rock has
so far been able to deliver us.


## 6


a lonely pine tree
on a hilltop miles away
resists the gathering leer
of the rock.

      Circling birds, warm
air rising, housetop TV aerials,
and wood smoke in streaks above
the rows of chimneys partly obscure
the tree's conical shape;
its millions of needles cannot
each be seen at all.  They will not
project on the rock's tiny screen.

in a true idea of synthesis, large
is found in small, complexity
hides simple, and distances
obscure reduction.

      Up to now,

fine coincidence of angle
and light has defined the standpoint
of the rock; the seashells were
perfect, too, companions
in illusion, motionless and solid,
yet happy to pass through the glass.

but, we have not been scrupulous
enough about cupboards
or picket fences. We have ignored,
in the excitement of shattering boundaries,
the obvious limitations of the rock's
field of view.
                Everyone's eye had overreached.

with these troubling observations
we have achieved a turning point.
the story's true; the last rays
from reclining Helios (not even
a rock can look straight
into the sun) cool obliquely
off the white paint of the fence,
cool flames in the window's
bold returning stare.

the shells grow anxious.
the walls come in close.

*"Everything is just an idea,"*
was thought all round.

                The rock failed
to hold the fractious light
in lifelike image, the beholder's
visual field  all reduced to changing
photons, into bare neural impulse,
making inferences from what
others had said they'd seen.

distant objects are, perhaps, best

drawn, then, in the mind's eye.
To enter into the cave of the mind,
the world must become a dream.
Rock walls intrude uncouthly,
but interpretations and design
are dreamed.

        No properly
animated rock would continue
to prefer geometry to process,
or give preference to sine
and cosine once he'd known
the asymmetric shrubs and crooked
cupboard doors, or the fine
irregular squiggles rough soles
have randomly scratched on
the checkerboard linoleum.

the rock is moving on just so,
abandoning straight lines
and perfect parallelograms, isosceles
triangles, regular zigzags,
and logarithmic curlicues.

*"Let the the rock be sentient!"*
the audience chants. *"We need a thinker
to imagine needles, who will
let us see their impossibly
excruciating distant thinness."*


**7**


pondered deeply, our thinking
reveals it lineage in flesh,
how it was always birthed
behind closed skulls.  Along
the atom-to-atom circuitry, chemical
reactions pile up, a cluster
here, a sinewy string of connections,

there; absence and presence, stuff
cluttering the doorway, well-lit
garden gates and pitch darkness.

such a lot is going on.

shadow and light play
in tangles over the retina;
synthesis-choosing metabolic
pathways down the cell-morass
of nerve and cerebral fluids.

isomerized draperies of purple
and violet, waving rods
and cones, linked beyond wet
surfaces, bravely running
neuron rapids to the cortex.

it is all the same with seeing;
clusters of electric charge
positioned like infielders
on the trusting retina, where
the brain extrudes part of its inward
workings to the outward
like a hernia; just so that
inside and out connect
on the mica layers of our rock's
eye, on its flat reflecting
side.   It picks up light waves
and reworks them. If a hair
is missing from a well-known
ear, the conceptual apparatus fills
it in; the same with pine needles.
the general idea spiffs up
the fragmentary thing.

                    Experience
makes metaphors from our
stimulated nerves and the secretions
washing in waves over brain

cells. Changes of temperature
and the rhythms of discharge
turn into hatred, logical relations,
a bad chill.
        The scientist probes
the one, devising machines to manifest
the unseen goings on; the poet
dresses up in the tattered others,
rummaging for lacey brooches and
sepia albums with dried flowers and
obituaries cut from old newspapers.


## 8


the rock as poet, poetizing
rock (to complete the metaphor)
simulates without within
in both the crystals of its micaceous
window and deeply in the hard
granite below. It can conjure
what collides, rework whatever
dances on its screen.
it can make corrections
in obedience to theory where
observations might just not
confirm specifics.

        All this was
expected from the start,
the careful reader will allow;
we were always looking through
the rock's eyes.  Now the pine needles
are displayed for all to see.

the jar reaches round to caress
the seashells, the seashells
rub up against the glass,
each other and their reborn
hero rock.

        The rock makes and shows
movies on his little screen;
the camera dollies and tracks
in an ever widening gyre.

until now no one had noticed
a defect in the mica, on the lower
left-hand corner of the little
squarish mirror, just a tiny chip
that marks a blind spot,
a hole in the rock's retina.  It shows
up first as a blur on the edge
of the closest huddling mollusk,
causes a bend in the third fence
picket from the left, but goes
unnoticed up in the clouds,
where details roll, spread,
                and swirl, anyway.

Anyway,
it's just a quirk that makes
the rock's world entirely
the rock's own; the rock's theories
are rock theories.  Undeterred,
the rock just detours round its chip.


**9**


now, we have humane intelligence
performed by a reproducing rock
picked up from a brook where
it had tumbled, probably,
for several lifetimes.

                It can
see anything as far as
there's good reason to see,
though an imperfection
nicked into its glassy edge

drives the eye to replicate
an error in each successive
scaling; progress and increase
are thus bought with ever
magnified distortion.

the goal was, absolutely
from the start, to see the swirls
etched in the pearly core
curvature of seashells in the jar
and then reflected in the shape
of the assembled stars (maybe
to discern the milky way, and
with it, God's own plan,
in the nacre inlay mirrored
in half a clam).

          What the rock
lusted after was much more
than merely sight and sense;
it strove for knowledge,
some certitude how everything
was governed, how each and every
part imbued the whole.

in the passing of Time,
the immense distances reaching
always toward us, fold over
themselves along a fault line,
a cosmic curtain wafting
in celestial breezes. Undulations
fan from dead center
to the edge, from large and near
to small and far, and the reverse,
exhibiting the infinite
in all its insignificance.

to the rock, what has happened
might all have been predicted;
the shape of the world resembling

familiar whorls inside familiar
seashells. All worlds grow, the gods
from rows of planted teeth;
everything unfolds until it
runs up against our stone's
idiosyncrasies—our philosophies
will then certainly mount up.

## **10**

### ***The Philosophy of the Rock, I***

*this rock* considered farthest worlds
subject to its mirror. They could be
dragged into the jar, put under glass.

remote was just another instance
of close by. If it fits into
the mirror, how strange could
it be? How hard to understand?
the shells themselves had never
moved of their own accord; sometimes
the jar was jostled or revolved,
and shells appeared at odd angles.

the rock's sweeping gaze edited
the jockeying calcite matrices
composing tableaux framed to
show only their very best sides,
oil on water spreading rainbows
of soft violet, blue, and pink.
when the sun stood just above
the picket fence, and the rain
had gone, the rock could paint seashell
patterns in the sky, could imagine
clouds as *trompe l'oeil* bowls
of fruit, could fashion mythic war
chariots, the mirages of their
steam-snorting horses quivering

in a rising patch of pale blue sky.

in the rock's mind the world
gave up its secrets in the mirror,
what the mirror could imagine.
from familiar to odd and weird is farther
than the distance traveled back,
when we hold our discoveries in old
cloth sacks sewn from common
knowledge. Nothing was entirely new.
blue light off the pretty shells,
bent oddly as we know (don't forget
the imperfection on the mirror's face,
that unseeing smidgen), so the farther
away it surveyed, the farther the rock's
estimates were off.
                    The larger errors
presently began to haunt the intimates
within the jar.  No shell was long
allowed to mean just what it meant.
shells became embodiments of vaster
implications; they wrongly stood
for more.
              The rock could not turn
to face away from any blemished shell,
could not ignore an imperfection
(it was powerless in that regard),
it could not move nor could it see
just how it wrongly saw, so it read
less meaning in the places its own
reflection spread.
                  Those sad stars
received the names of lesser deities
          —panic, narcissism, cupidity.
in the rock's garden, they were simply
moved into the shade, where
they vied with the dying lilies.

## 11

### *The Philosophy of the Rock, II*

there are two senses, the rock
avers, of center; the jar
that holds the rock and the rock itself.

the rock contains the world,
and the jar holds the rock,
but cannot hold the rock's roving
eye.  Knowing no limits, the rock
imagines also God in two persons,
one that does, and another
that makes possible.
                         The rock
is the moving center,
going where it sees things
on the cracked, distorted glass,
inventing fabulous objects
and creatures, three-winged
blackbirds pecking insects
on a twisting fence, or rooftops
droopy in the center, bowed with
                         imaginary weight.
The jar is the center that holds still.

what moves, is then moving
around it.
                See it and you are
justified and can thus understand
how to drag objects under the lens
                and read out each's name—
*"fence, flower, shell, cloud, star,"*
edicts from proclaimed divinity,
vain and arrogant, insisting
Time and Motion owe their Being
to its Will (the rock in the jar).

no other Genesis is countenanced.

word gets around—the Cat is out.

the fence was created for shade
infrequently dappled in dark
and lighter stripes along the flowers;
the flowers were born from the need
for a capricious yellow offered
up to the rock.
                The clouds
and the stars among them sing
a music silent in the yard,
heard only by the rock itself
                    within the jar;
the cracks are plastered
up with mysteries. *"listen. . . ."*
the rock begins to hum.

some excess energy blows as wind
through a whistle-notched reed,
hardly audible at first, but soon
a rattling is noticed among
the seashells, sending brittle echoes
along the curved glass of the jar.
the table sways in sympathy
and the whistling, ever shriller,
passes through the windows to the yard,
past the fence, into the waiting sky.

as if the world had been tapped
like a tuning fork, the pitch
infects glass, rock, wood, plant,
and stars.
               They squirm in oscillating
rhythms—No one can sleep.


**12**


the action in the jar intrudes
impossibly into your own restless

tossing in the noisy, jar-shaking
night.  Culpability awakes and wakes
you and in you, makes you stare
into the blackness.
                              The night
hangs slack in the windows,
but the rock glows in your mind's
eye, threatening reason
and routine with its anarchy.

*"I've got to put it back,"*
you whisper, coming up from sleep.
*"Something's very wrong."*
*"Put what back?"* your wife wants to know.
*"The rock,"* you say, *"the rock I stole*
*from its place in the stream bed."*
*"Oh, that's silly; go back to sleep."*

instead, you get up quickly and dress.
In the kitchen everything
is quiet.  Some invisible token
of calamity remains, but you can't
be sure.  The whole room,
the windows, and the yard outside
are holding their breath.

you pick up the jar, walk to the sink,
twist the lid, and smelly water
pours through your fingers
along with seashells, till you have
only the rock, so small, inert
in your hand; it goes into
your pocket and weighs a ton
by the time you've hiked
and found the pool.

                              The exact
desecrated site discovered,
an obvious hollow the size
of the errant rock in the sandy

bottom of the stream.  Surrounding
rocks gape blindly, oblivious
to dull shapes and shadows,
waiting in perpetual obscurity,
dead to the spreading dawn.

you go down on one knee to refit
the stone, face up, like a glass eye
in its socket.
                        It barely glances,
but you catch the wet suggestion
of yourself as the rock sees you.

the fracture on the layered mica
surface twists your cameo,
making your right eye enlarge fiercely;
then it's gone.
                        The tumbling
stream rolls the rock over
on its face, its unseeing granite
backside facing upwards now.


*An earlier prose version of this poem first appeared
   in *Gone Lawn,* 32 (Winter Solstice, 2022).

www.ingramcontent.com/pod-product-compliance
Lightning Source LLC
Chambersburg PA
CBHW061223210726

48294CB00006B/1955